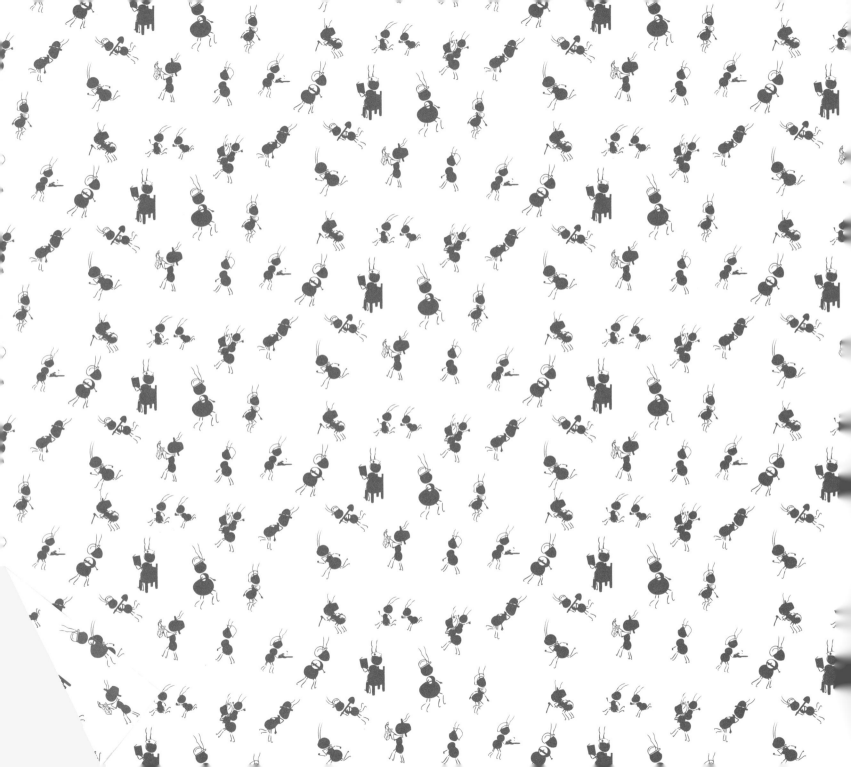

Alex the Ant Goes to the BEACH

Written by Eric Wayne Dickey   Illustrated by Abbey Paccia

First Edition June 2014.

Cover and interior design by Brian David Smith
Cover illustration by Abbey Paccia

_____

Library of Congress Cataloging-in-Publication Data

Dickey, Eric Wayne, 1967-
 Alex the ant goes to the beach / written by Eric Wayne Dickey; illustrated by Abbey Paccia. --
First edition.
     pages cm
 Summary: When Alex accompanies older ants to the beach on his first trip outside of
Underwood, he enjoys playing but also demonstrates that he will one day be a great scout for
Queen Aziza when he alerts the work crew to danger.
 ISBN 978-1-940052-08-3 (alk. paper)
 [1. Ants--Fiction.] I. Paccia, Abbey, illustrator. II. Title.

PZ7.D5577Ale 2014
[E]--dc23

                          2014001319
_____

Printed in Malaysia

ISBN: 978-1-940052-08-3

CRAIGMORE CREATIONS

Portland, OR
www.craigmorecreations.com

For Andy Still.
Dedicated to Allen and Ava.
-Eric Wayne Dickey

For my family.
-Abbey Paccia

"Oh, boy! Oh, boy!" exclaimed Alex as he got out of bed.
"I'm going to the beach today!"

The older ants were going to work at the beach. One of the scout ants had found something good to bring back to the Underwood anthill. The older ants thought it would be a good opportunity to bring the young scout with them. And the queen had agreed.

"It's time the young scout ventured out of Underwood," Queen Aziza proclaimed while patting Alex on the head.

Alex stood mesmerized in Queen Aziza's stately presence, but inside, he wiggled with joy. When he grows up, he hopes to be the best scout ant the queen and the Underwood anthill have ever had.

Alex ran back to his room to get the backpack he had already prepared for his trip to the beach.

A scout ant is always prepared for adventure.

The anthill is an amazing maze of short passageways and long tunnels. Alex loved to run through them. He ran past the ant nurseries. He ran past the food storage rooms, and he ran back to his resting chamber.

He plopped on his sailor hat, put on his favorite striped shirt, and packed a beach blanket into his backpack. He was ready to go.

As he was weaving his way out through Underwood's amazing tunnels, one of the oldest ants, Aloysius, stopped Alex.

"Beware of the waves," said Aloysius.

Aloysius was Underwood's aging sea captain. He had a patch over his eye, a long gray beard, and a raspy voice—a whalebone pipe hung from his mouth. He had been to sea many times and once had an accident that left him with a wooden leg. Alex shuddered when he looked down at the peg leg.

"The waves can sneak up behind you before you know it. Beware!" Aloysius called out as Alex hurried off, his voice echoing throughout the Underwood ant tunnels. "Beware!"

Alex was running so fast, he shot from the top of Underwood like a cannonball. The work crew had already begun marching.

"Hurry up, Alex!" they called.

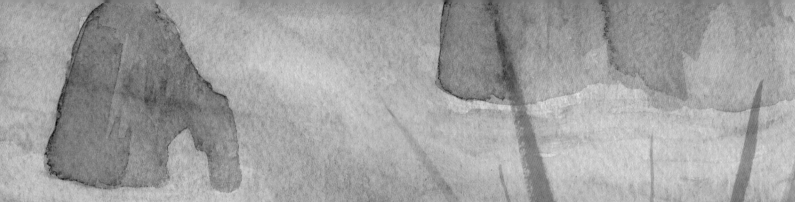

It was easy for Alex to follow the other ants because ants leave a scent trail wherever they go. Ants can smell the scent trails with their antennae. Even though Alex lagged behind, the older ants didn't worry. Alex would follow the scent trail and eventually find the others. And so he did.

Not long after Alex joined the back of the line of ants, the front of the line arrived at its destination. The ants began to take apart a piece of wood that had been soaking in water for a long time. It was easy to take apart.

"Why does Underwood need that?" Alex asked the worker ants as they passed by. One of them, George, started to answer, but he was carrying a piece of wood in his mandibles, so his answer sounded like he was talking with his mouth full of food. "Mee nee it too eet," said George.

Alex looked puzzled. George put down the wood he was carrying. It took him a second to catch his breath.

"We need it to eat," George started to answer again.

Another ant came from behind and grumbled something with his full mandible. It sounded like, "Mmm mm ha da may!" Which Alex took to mean, "Get out of the way!" or maybe, "We don't have all day!"

George continued to explain. "We put this deep in underground rooms so it can grow the yummy mold we love to eat."

"Yummy mold?!" Alex thought to himself.

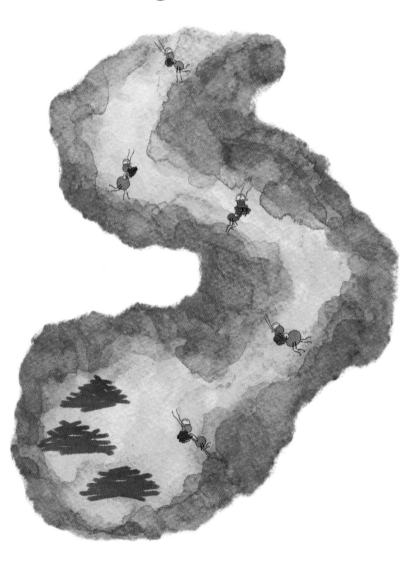

George, a timid fellow, felt the glares of others, so he picked up a few pieces of wood with his mandibles and scrambled back in line, saying, "Mmm tol ew suh mo lader!" which Alex understood as, "I'll tell you some more later!"

The older ants asked Alex to stay on the lookout to keep the ants safe while they worked. Alex found a nice sunny spot on the beach, next to a big rock close to the work site. He pulled out his blanket; it fluttered and rippled as he spread it out on the sand. He heard the sound of ocean waves. Being a natural scout, he wanted to get a closer look at the ocean.

He found a small tide pool and floated around it on a twig. He made believe he was a sailor ant aboard a big ship and yelled out, "Aye, aye, skipper," and, "Walk the plank!" and various other sailor-type sayings. While floating around the tide pool, Alex looked down into the water. He saw clams and barnacles. He even saw an anemone and a sea star. Suddenly, Alex saw a fish swim toward him. It nearly tipped over Alex's twig boat. He quickly paddled back to shore.

Alex jumped back onto solid ground and looked around for his scent trail. Without a scent trail an ant can get lost. His trail must have been washed away. Alex started to panic.

Alex remembered Aloysius's warning, his peg leg, and echoing voice.

At that moment, Alex heard the sound of water. He turned around to look behind him and saw a wave rushing toward him. It nearly swept him up, but Alex was a fast little guy. He ran faster than the wave, despite the foam falling on his feet.

Once Alex was far enough away from the reach of the waves, he put his antennae to the ground and zigzagged back and forth, searching for the scent trail. He eventually found it and made his way back to where the crew was working.

"You shouldn't wander off too far. Stay close," the older ants scolded.

One of the older scout ants, Ishmael, brought over his prized possession—a collapsible telescope. He asked Alex to hold it for him. The other ants needed Ishmael to help move a big piece of wood.

Alex climbed atop the big rock by his blanket and pretended to be a sailor in the crow's nest of a tall ship. He yelled out "Land, ho!" as he peered through the spyglass.

He pointed the telescope over the water and was amazed at the ocean's size. He saw waves breaking on the beach and he saw boats way off shore. "I wonder if there are any ants on those boats," he thought to himself.

He spied around some more with the telescope and turned to look up and down the beach. Just then, he saw a big, slobbery dog with a big, slobbery ball in its big, slobbery mouth running toward him and the work crew.

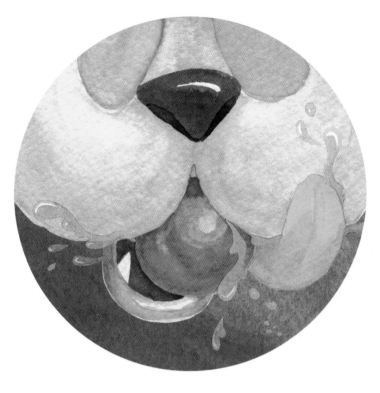

"Thar she blows!" he whispered, because he couldn't believe what he was seeing and because he was scared of getting stepped on by the dog. He quickly scrambled down his make-believe ship and scurried back to the work site.

Nearly out of breath, he blurted out, "There's a big, slobbery dog coming this way!"

Without hesitating, one of the worker ants, Sherman, yelled, "Everybody, go underground! Now!"

And just like magic, all the working ants stopped what they were doing and scuttled down into any nook and cranny or crevice they could find. Some went under twigs, others under leaves, and others just froze right where they were standing. Sherman pulled Alex beneath a rock just as the dog passed over. One big paw stepped right where Alex and Sherman had been standing, and was followed by one big glop of slobbery dog goo.

"That was a close one!" Sherman said with a sigh of relief.

All the ants resurfaced and cheered: "Hooray for Alex! Alex saved the day!"

By that time the job was nearly finished, and fewer and fewer ants were returning to the work site. Someone said, "Let's go home, everybody."

Alex packed his blanket into his backpack and stepped back into the line of ants marching home to Underwood.

He returned the spyglass to Ishmael. "Thanks for letting me hold it."

"No, you keep it," said Ishmael. "You're going to be a great scout! I can tell."

Alex beamed with pride.

After arriving home and having a
tasty dinner of sweet mold (sweet
mold?!), Alex fell asleep fast. He'd
had a big day.

That night, he dreamt of waves and
sunsets, of sea gulls and whales, and
of a big ship with a round sea captain
who said, "Ahoy thar matey!" and
"Welcome aboard!"

The End.

Eric Wayne Dickey is a writer and a father. His poetry has been widely published and anthologized. He lives in Oregon with his wife, a K12 science teacher. Together they tend a huge garden and are raising two children. This is his first children's book.

Illustrator Abbey Paccia grew up in Central New York, where she developed a love of nature and stories. Abbey has worked as an animator, storyboard artist, and illustrator. Alongside her commercial work, she is currently writing a series of fantasy novels set in a fictional land much inspired by the mountains and forests of Oregon.